Ladybird Readers

The Wind in the Willows

 To download full story audio in both British and American accents, and to complete the listening activities at the back of the book, visit **www.ladybirdeducation.co.uk**

Contents

Ladybird Readers

The Wind
in the Willows

6 976 384 000

Series Editor: Sorrel Pitts
Text adapted by Sorrel Pitts
Illustrated by Ester García-Cortés

LADYBIRD BOOKS

UK | USA | Canada | Ireland | Australia
India | New Zealand | South Africa

Ladybird Books is part of the Penguin Random House group of companies
whose addresses can be found at global.penguinrandomhouse.com.
www.penguin.co.uk   www.puffin.co.uk   www.ladybird.co.uk

Penguin
Random House
UK

First published 2018
001

Copyright © Ladybird Books Ltd, 2018

Printed in China

A CIP catalogue record for this book is available from the British Library

ISBN: 978-0-241-33613-7

All correspondence to
Ladybird Books
Penguin Random House Children's
80 Strand, London WC2R 0RL

MIX
Paper from
responsible sources
FSC
www.fsc.org   FSC® C018179

Characters

Mole

Rat

Toad

Badger

weasels

prison manager's
daughter

boat woman

CHAPTER ONE

At the River

Mole was cleaning his little house when he looked out of the window and saw that it was a warm spring day.

"It's too nice to be inside," he said to himself.

So, he stopped cleaning, and walked to the river. On the other side of the river, he saw a water rat.

"Hello, Mr. Mole," said the rat. "Would you like to come on my boat?"

"Hello, Mr. Rat," said Mole. "Yes, I think I will."

So, Rat sailed his little boat to Mole.

"I love having fun on boats," said Rat. "I've got a big picnic here, too. We can eat it later."

"This is all wonderful!" said Mole.

Then, Rat saw Mole looking at a **huge*** forest.

"That's the Wild Forest," said Rat. "I don't like it because it's full of weasels. Although, Mr. Badger lives there, too, and he is quite nice. So is Mr. Toad at Toad Hall, but he likes cars too much!"

CHAPTER TWO

Mole and Rat Become Friends

Rat took Mole to his house.

"I like your house, Mr. Rat," said Mole.

"How about staying here until the summer?" Rat asked.

"I'd like that, thank you," replied Mole.

Mole was feeling very happy later that night, when he went to bed in Rat's **comfortable** home.

The next day, Rat took Mole to visit Toad at Toad Hall. It was a very **grand** building, and it had a huge garden.

Toad was very happy because he had a new horse and **caravan**.

"Let's take the caravan somewhere," he said.

So, they took the horse and caravan out for a journey.

Not far from Toad Hall, a very grand car suddenly drove past very quickly. The horse became frightened, and the caravan fell over.

Toad didn't mind. He was watching the car.

"I want that car," he said.

Chapter Three

Badger

It was winter now, and Mole was still staying with Rat.

One day, Mole thought, "I've heard a lot about Mr. Badger, so I must meet him."

Mole walked into the Wild Forest, but it was **frightening**. It was full of animals, and there were strange noises.

Rat saw Mole walk into the forest and he felt worried, so he followed him. Together, they walked to Badger's house.

Badger gave them a **delicious** dinner, and they talked about how much Toad loved cars.

"We must talk to Mr. Toad about his cars," said Badger. "I'm worried. He drives too fast."

In the morning, they all had a nice breakfast. Then, Badger walked with Mole and Rat to the edge of the forest.

CHAPTER FOUR
Mole Goes Home

Later in the winter, Mole and Rat decided to go for a walk.

Soon, Mole came to a place that he knew, and he smelled a smell that he knew, too.

"We're near my home!" he told Rat. "I want to go there."

They soon found Mole's old home. The house was very untidy, and Rat was hungry.

"Will there be any food?" Rat said to himself.

Mole tidied the house while Rat looked in the cupboards, where he found biscuits and some cans of fish.

"Great!" Rat said. "We have lots to eat!"

So, they had a delicious dinner of biscuits and fish, and then they slept in a pair of comfortable beds.

Mole was feeling very happy, because he was back in his own house with his best friend, Rat.

CHAPTER FIVE

Toad's Problem

Soon, it was spring again. Badger came to visit Rat and Mole, but he wasn't very happy.

"It's Mr. Toad," he said. "We have to do something about him. He loves cars too much, and it's making **trouble** for him with the police."

So, the three friends went to visit Toad at Toad Hall. Very soon, they saw their friend. He was sitting in a big car.

"Come with me for a drive!" he said.

"You're not driving anywhere," said Badger.

That didn't stop Toad, who quickly drove away in his car! He drove along a road, and, suddenly, he saw a very grand car outside a restaurant.

"I want to drive *that* car," thought Toad, so he got in it.

Suddenly, the police came. They **arrested** Toad, and put him in prison.

who

Chapter Six

Toad Escapes

The prison **manager**'s daughter liked animals, and she felt sorry for Toad.

"These are my aunt's clothes," she said. "Put them on now, and then I will help you escape. If anyone stops you, you must **pretend** you are a poor **washer woman**."

"Thank you," said Toad, and he left the prison.

Toad went to the train station, but he couldn't buy a ticket because he didn't have any money.

Then, he saw a train driver. "If you give me a **lift**, I'll wash your shirts for you," Toad said.

The train driver agreed.

Suddenly, they saw another train behind them, with lots of angry police on it. They were following Toad!

"Oh no! I'm in trouble," Toad said to the train driver. "I stole a car. Please stop, so that I can escape."

The train driver stopped the train, and Toad jumped off.

CHAPTER SEVEN

The Boat Woman

Toad was near to his home when he came to a big river. There, he met a boat woman.

"Please can I have a lift on your boat?" he asked.

"You can have a lift if you wash my clothes," she answered. Toad agreed, and he got on the boat.

The boat woman gave him lots of dirty clothes to wash.

"I'm sorry, but I don't know how to wash them," said Toad.

"You lied to me! You are not a washer woman, you're an ugly toad!" shouted the boat woman. "Get off my boat!"

So, Toad jumped off the boat, and he started walking again.

A short time later, a car came toward him. It was the same grand car that he had stolen from the restaurant!

Toad immediately made a plan. He pretended to **faint**, and fell to the ground.

Chapter Eight

In the Pond

The car stopped, and the people got out.

"Have you fainted?" they asked, in worried
voices. Toad opened his eyes and nodded.

"Let us give you a lift home, you poor
washer woman."

Toad smiled to himself, and got into the car.

Soon, Toad pretended he felt better.
"This is a very grand car," he said.
"Please may I drive it?"

The people thought this idea was funny—
a washer woman driving a car!

So, Toad got into the driver's seat. He drove slowly at first, and then a bit faster.

"Please drive more slowly," said the people in the car.

"I am not a washer woman!" said Toad. Then, he drove too fast around a corner, and the car went into a **pond**.

Toad jumped from the car, and began to swim. Suddenly, he saw a face under the water. It was Rat!

CHAPTER NINE

A Problem at Toad Hall

Rat took Toad to his home, and dried him with a towel.

"While you were in prison, the weasels from the forest went to live in Toad Hall!" Rat told him, angrily. "They won't let you back in there."

When he heard this news, Toad began to cry. At that moment, Badger and Mole arrived. They were very happy to see Toad, who started to tell them all about his adventures in a **proud** voice.

"Stop talking about yourself, Mr. Toad!" said Badger. "You have been very bad—you mustn't be proud about that!"

When he heard these words, Toad began to cry again.

"I have a plan to make the weasels leave your house," said Rat. "They are having a party tomorrow to **celebrate** taking Toad Hall. There is a **tunnel** under the house. We will go through it and give them a **surprise**!"

CHAPTER TEN

The Party

The four friends had dinner, then they went to Toad Hall.

They walked through the tunnel until they were under Toad's house. Now, they could hear one of the weasels who was at the party. He was singing a funny song about Toad, and cars, and prison.

"Let me attack him!" said Toad, angrily.

"Yes, let's go!" cried Badger, and the four friends ran into the room where the weasels were sitting around the dinner table.

The weasels jumped from their chairs with surprise. There was a big fight, and then the weasels ran back into the forest!

Toad decided to have a big dinner party to celebrate.

"Now, I want to tell you all about myself, and my adventures," he said, proudly.

"No!" said Mole and Badger, angrily. "You must start thinking about other people first."

CHAPTER ELEVEN
Toad's Lesson

So, Toad went upstairs, and sang one last song about himself. Then, he came back downstairs.

"Well done, my friends," he said. "Well done, Rat, for having the idea, and well done, all of you, for frightening the weasels. It was your work, not mine."

Next, Toad sent money to the prison manager's daughter. He also wanted to pay for his lifts, so he sent presents to the train driver, the boat woman, and the people who were in the grand car.

Toad never again spoke about himself in a proud voice.

The four animals often went for walks together along the river. They enjoyed eating big picnics on Rat's boat, and sometimes they went driving in Toad's grand cars, but he never drove too fast!

They were happy. It was good to have friends.

Activities

The activities at the back of this book help you to practice the following skills:

Spelling and writing

Reading

Speaking

Listening

Critical thinking

Preparation for the Cambridge Young Learners exams

1 **Look at the picture and read the questions. Write the answers in your notebook.**

1 Whose boat is it?

2 Who does he invite on to his boat?

3 What are they going to eat later?

4 Where do the weasels live?

2 **You are Mole. Ask and answer the questions with a friend, using the words in the box.**

> Badger boat forest walking warm

1 What were you doing when you saw Rat?

2 What was the weather like?

3 Where was Rat?

4 What were you looking at when you were on the boat?

5 Who did Rat think was quite nice?

3 **Read the sentences. If a sentence is not correct, write the correct sentence in your notebook.** 📖 ✏️

1   Mole didn't like Rat's house.

2   Mole wasn't feeling very happy later that night, when he went to bed.

3   Toad Hall was a very grand building.

4   Toad Hall didn't have a big garden.

4 **Read the text, and write all the text with the correct verbs in your notebook.** 📖 ✏️

The next day, Rat . . . (**take**) Mole to visit Toad at Toad Hall. Toad . . . (**be**) very happy because he . . . (**have**) a new horse and caravan. "Let's take the caravan somewhere," he . . . (**say**). So, they . . . (**take**) the horse and caravan out for a journey. Not far from Toad Hall, a very grand car suddenly . . . (**drive**) past very quickly. The horse . . . (**become**) frightened, and the caravan . . . (**fall**) over. Toad did not mind. He . . . (**watch**) the car.

5 **Choose the correct words, and write the full sentences in your notebook.** 📖 ✏️ 💬

1	autumn	summer	winter
2	week	day	minute
3	noises	smells	tastes

1 It was . . . now, and Mole was still staying with Rat.

2 One . . . , Mole thought, "I've heard a lot about Mr. Badger, so I must meet him."

3 Mole walked into the Wild Forest, but it was frightening. It was full of animals, and there were strange . . .

6 **Listen to Chapter Three. Answer the questions below in your notebook.** 🎧*✏️

1 Why was Rat worried?

2 What did he do?

3 Where did they go?

4 What did Badger give them?

5 What did they talk about?

*To complete this activity, listen to track 4 of the audio download available at www.ladybirdeducation.co.uk

7 Work with a friend. Talk about the two pictures. How are they different?

a

b

In picture a, Badger, Rat, and Mole are sitting at the table.

In picture b, Rat and Mole are tidying Mole's house.

8 Choose the correct words, and write the full sentences in your notebook.

1 Later in the winter, Mole and Rat decided **go / to go** for a walk.

2 Soon, Mole **came / came to** a place that he knew, and he smelled a smell that he knew, too.

3 "We're near my home!" he told Rat. "I want **go / to go** there."

4 Mole's house was very untidy, and Rat was hungry. "Will there be any food?" Rat said **to him. / to himself.**

9 **Read the answers, and write the questions in your notebook.** 📖 ✏️

    1 It was spring.

    2 Badger came to visit Rat and Mole.

    3 Because he was worried about Toad.

    4 He loved cars too much.

    5 It was making trouble with the police.

10 **Describe Toad in your own words in your notebook.** ✏️ ❓

11 **Choose the correct answers, and write the full sentences in your notebook.**

1 The . . . daughter liked animals.
   a boat woman's   **b** prison manager's
   c policeman's   **d** train driver's

2 Toad pretended to be a . . .
   a mole.   **b** rat.
   c washer woman.   **d** weasel.

3 Toad wanted a . . .
   a break.   **b** lift.
   c meal.   **d** wash.

4 Toad stole . . .
   a a car.   **b** a caravan.
   c a train.   **d** some clothes.

12 **Ask and answer the questions with a friend.**

1 *Why did the prison manager's daughter help Toad?*

Because she liked animals, and she felt sorry for him.

2 What did she do to help him?

3 How did Toad get the train driver to help him?

4 Who was on the train behind Toad's train?

13 **Read the questions. In your notebook, write answers in full sentences using words in the box.**

lift   car   wash   boat woman

dirty clothes   lie

1   Who did Toad meet by the river?

2   How did she help him?

3   What did Toad have to do?

4   What did the boat woman give Toad?

5   Why was she angry with him?

6   What was coming toward Toad?

14 **Rewrite Chapter Seven as a play script.**

Toad is standing next to a big river.
A boat woman is in her boat on the river.

Toad: Please can I have a lift in your boat?

15 **Listen to the definitions. Write the correct word from Chapter One in your notebook. 🎧***

1 arrest / celebrate / faint / pretend

2 caravan / lift / tunnel / trouble

3 boat woman / police / prison manger / washer woman

4 grand / frightening / delicious / comfortable

5 pond / pretend / proud / river

16 **Talk to a friend about Toad's plan. Ask and answer questions. 💬**

Why did Toad pretend to faint?

So he could get a lift in the grand car.

17 **Read the information. Choose the correct names, and write them in your notebook.**

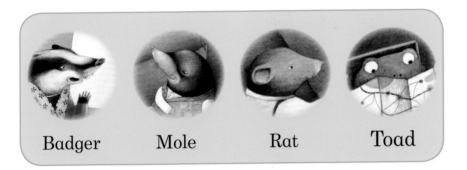

| Badger | Mole | Rat | Toad |

1 He's very proud, and he likes driving fast.

2 He can swim well, and he has got a boat.

3 He lives in the Wild Forest, and he is tall and quite nice.

4 He likes cleaning, and he can smell very well.

18 **Write some instructions in your notebook to help Toad get the weasels out of Toad Hall.**

1. Find the tunnel at Toad Hall . . .

19 **Match the two parts of the sentences. Write the full sentences in your notebook.**

1 They walked through the tunnel

2 The four friends ran into the room

3 There was a big fight,

a and then the weasels ran back into the forest!

b until they were under Toad's house.

c where the weasels were sitting around the dinner table.

20 **Look at the picture and write sentences about it using *anyone*, *anybody*, *everyone*, *someone*, or *no one* in your notebook.**

1. Someone is not fighting.

21 **Read the text below. Find the five mistakes, and write the correct text in your notebook.**

Toad sent money to the washer woman. He also wanted to pay for his lifts, so he sent presents to the train driver, the boat woman, and the people who were in Toad Hall.

He always spoke about himself in a proud voice.

The four animals often went for walks together along the river. They hated having dinner at Toad Hall, and sometimes they went driving in Toad's grand cars, but he never drove too fast!

They were hungry. It was good to have friends.

22 **You are Toad. Write a thank-you letter from Toad to Rat at the end of the story.**

Dear Rat,

I want to say thank you for helping me . . .

Project

Look online, or in the library, and find out about an animal who lives in the forest.

Make a poster about the animal. Work in a group. Include the information below:

- What is the animal called?

- Where does it live?

- How big is it?

- What does it eat?

- What does it do?

Glossary

arrest *(verb)*
when police take a person to a police station and keep them there, because they believe the person has done something wrong

caravan *(noun)*
a small house with wheels, pulled by a horse or car

celebrate *(verb)*
to do something special to show that a day or time is important

comfortable *(adjective)*
When you are warm and happy, you are *comfortable.*

delicious (adjective)
When food or drink is really nice, it is *delicious.*

faint *(verb)*
to fall down suddenly and not be awake

frightening *(adjective)*
When something makes you feel frightened, it is *frightening.*

grand *(adjective)*
When something is big and expensive, it is *grand.*

huge *(adjective)*
When something is very big, it is *huge.*

lift *(noun)*
When you take someone from one place to another in a car, you give them a *lift.*

manager *(noun)*
a person who controls a business, a place, or a team

pond *(noun)*
A small place outside that is full of water. Sometimes, there are fish in a pond.

pretend *(verb)*
When you act like something that you are not, you *pretend*.

proud *(adjective)*
When you feel happy with yourself, you are *proud*.

surprise *(noun)*
A *surprise* is something that happens to make someone feel surprised.

trouble *(noun)*
A difficult or dangerous problem. If you are in *trouble*, the police may arrest you.

tunnel *(noun)*
a path in a hole under the ground

washer woman *(noun)*
a woman whose job is to wash clothes

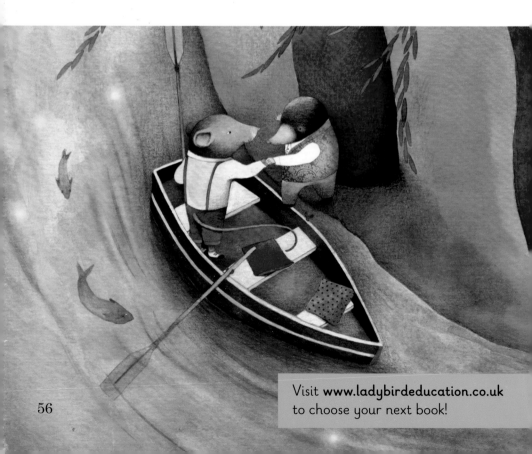

Visit **www.ladybirdeducation.co.uk** to choose your next book!